THIS BOOK BELONGS TO:

_____

_____

_____

_____

To my Worley-Bird, aka Jo-Lynne Worley – H.L.

To my husband, Aron Bernstein – S.G.

and to Phyllis Rubin, the *real* Aunt Phyllis – S.G. and H.L.

First published 2001 by Walker Books Ltd
87 Vauxhall Walk, London SE11 5HJ

This edition published 2002

10 9 8 7 6 5 4 3 2 1

Text © 2001 Harriet Lerner and Susan Goldhor
Illustrations © 2001 Helen Oxenbury

This book has been typeset in StempelGaramond

Produced by Hedgehog Books Ltd, Alton, England

Printed in Singapore by Tien Wah Press (Pte.) Ltd

British Library Cataloguing in Publication Data:
a catalogue record for this book is available from the British Library

ISBN 0-7445-8951-7

Franny B. Kranny
There's a Bird in your Hair!

Harriet Lerner & Susan Goldhor
illustrated by
Helen Oxenbury

WALKER BOOKS
AND SUBSIDIARIES
LONDON · BOSTON · SYDNEY

Franny B. Kranny had long frizzy hair.
It was always getting her into trouble.
Franny B. Kranny's hair tied itself in knots
on the buttons of her dress.

Franny B. Kranny's hair made the girl
sitting next to her on the school bus sneeze
every day on the way to school.

Franny B. Kranny's hair even got stuck in the fridge door.

But Franny B. Kranny loved her long frizzy hair. The longer and frizzier it got, the more she liked it.

Franny B. Kranny thought her long frizzy hair was beautiful. She could brush it down in front of her face and pretend she was in a cave.

She could press it flat
against her head and watch it
boing out again.

Franny B. Kranny's mother was very tired of untangling so much long frizzy hair.

"Wouldn't you like nice neat short pretty hair like your sister Bertha's?" she asked.

"No!" said Franny B. Kranny.

"I think you would look so pretty with short hair," said Franny B. Kranny's father.

"I think so too!" said Bertha.

"No!" said Franny B. Kranny.

One day Franny B. Kranny's parents announced
that there was going to be a big family party.
All their relations would be coming.

"And," said Franny B. Kranny's mother,
"the day before the party you are both going
to the hairdresser's."

"I'm going to get my hair curled," said Bertha proudly.

"I'm not," said Franny B. Kranny. "I don't want anyone touching my hair."

"We'll see," said Franny B. Kranny's mother.

Before she knew it, the day before the party had come. Franny B. Kranny's mother told the hairdresser exactly what she wanted him to do with Franny B. Kranny's hair.

"Pin it up on her head and make it neat," she said.

"You have very interesting hair, young lady," the hairdresser said politely. He had never seen anything like it before.

Franny B. Kranny didn't like him one bit. She closed her eyes, shut her mouth and crossed her arms. She didn't say a word to him all the time he worked on her hair.

"There!" said the hairdresser at last. "Don't you look pretty?"

Franny B. Kranny opened her eyes. Her long frizzy hair was piled on top of her head in a giant heap.

"Very nice," said her mother.

"At least it won't fly around and get caught in the cake," said Bertha.

Franny B. Kranny didn't say anything. She just stared into the mirror, thinking about the best way to undo her new hairdo.

Franny B. Kranny was walking slowly home behind her mother and Bertha, thinking and thinking, when suddenly something amazing happened. A brown bird flew down from a nearby tree and landed in the middle of Franny B. Kranny's new hairdo.

Her mother screamed and Bertha jumped up and down, but the bird would not budge. It just snuggled deeper into the pile of long frizzy hair on the top of Franny B. Kranny's head.

"Don't scare it away," said Franny B. Kranny. "I like it there."

When they reached their front door the brown bird was still there.

"Maybe it thinks you're a tree," said Franny B. Kranny's mother.

"Maybe it thinks your hair is a nest," said Bertha.

"There's a bird in your hair!" said Franny B. Kranny's father. "Maybe you should undo your new hairdo!"

Suddenly Franny B. Kranny began to like her new hairdo.

"No!" said Franny B. Kranny.

But at bedtime Franny B. Kranny had some problems to solve. How could she bend over to take off her shoes with a bird in her hair? Then she remembered the deep knee bends she had learned in her gym class.

How could she go to sleep with a bird in her hair? Then she remembered her father's big armchair. After everyone else had gone to sleep, she tiptoed down the hall and curled up in it.

In the morning there were more problems.

"Time for a shower!" said Franny B. Kranny's mother.

A shower! thought Franny B. Kranny. Oh, no! Instead she had a bath and was very careful not to splash water on her head.

Soon it was time for the family party. Bertha was very embarrassed to have a sister with a bird in her hair.

"I'm going to tell everyone that I've never seen Franny B. Kranny before in my life!" she told her parents.

"Birdbrain!" she said to Franny B. Kranny.

But Franny B. Kranny thought she looked
beautiful, and she marched proudly into the
party with the brown bird perched on the
very top of her hairdo.

No one at the family party had ever seen a hairdo like it! Everyone crowded around Franny B. Kranny.

Her cousin Ethan, who never smiled, laughed out loud when Franny B. Kranny let him feed the bird a peanut.

Uncle Isadore, who was usually very grouchy, told
Franny B. Kranny he was sorry he was bald and
couldn't take his favourite pigeon home from the park.
It would slide off his head!

Aunt Phyllis, who worked at a television station, thought Franny B. Kranny's hair was NEWS. She called her office and told them to send some cameras. Now Bertha stayed close to Franny B. Kranny. She wanted everyone to know they were sisters.

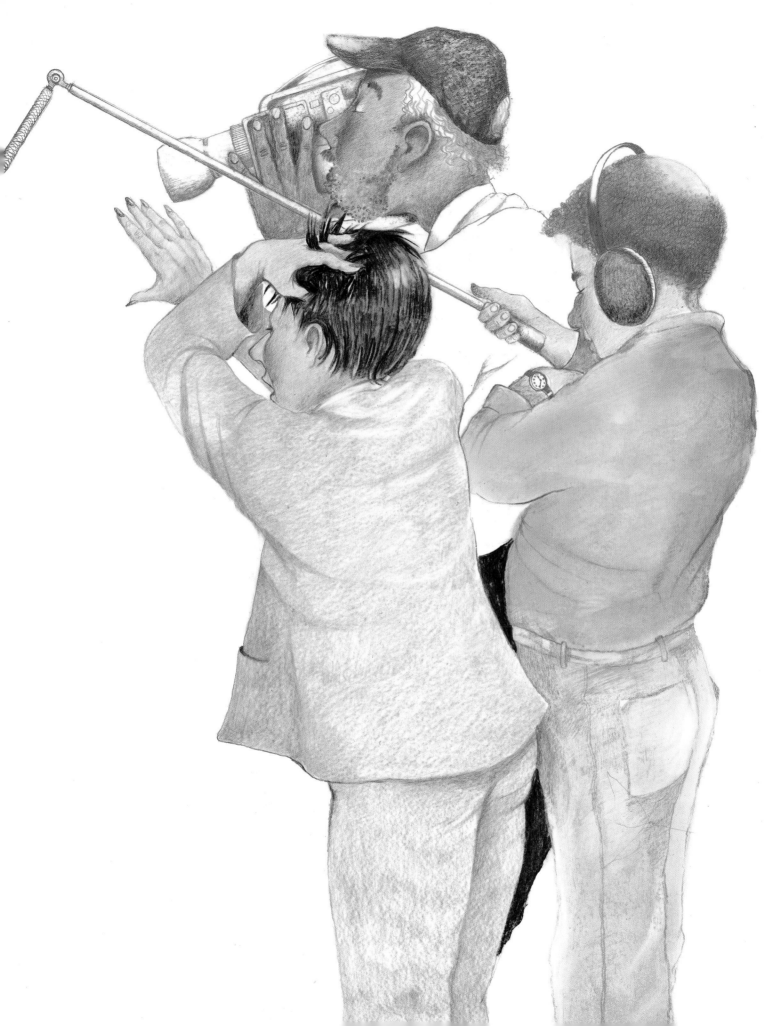

The day after the party Bertha said,
"I'm so glad you didn't cut your hair.
It's brilliant!"

"That's what you think!" said Franny
B. Kranny. "I'm getting it cut tomorrow."

"Oh no!" cried her mother. "You can't
do that!"

"Oh yes," said Franny B. Kranny, "I can."

"Why now?" asked her father.

"A little birdie told me to!" said Franny B. Kranny.

HARRIET LERNER and SUSAN GOLDHOR are sisters. Harriet is a respected authority on family relationships and has published several books on the subject. She and her husband live in Kansas, USA, and have two sons, Matt and Ben. Susan, Harriet's big sister, is a biologist. She lives in Massachusetts, USA, with her husband, who is a physicist.

HELEN OXENBURY is one of today's most established children's book illustrators. She has won many awards for her books, which include *Tickle, Tickle*; *Clap Hands*; the Tom and Pippo books; *Farmer Duck*; *We're Going on a Bear Hunt*; and *So Much*. Helen is married to illustrator John Burningham. They have three grown-up children and live in north London.